KT-584-400

Fife Council Education Department
King's Road Primary School
King's Crescent, Rosyth KY11 2RS

Ghost for Sale

by

Terry Deary

Illustrated by Steve Donald

You do not need to read this page - just get on with the book!

First published 1999 in Great Britain by
Barrington Stoke Ltd
10 Belford Terrace, Edinburgh, EH4 3DQ
Reprinted 1999 (three times)

This edition published 2001

Copyright © 1999, 2001 Terry Deary
Illustrations © Steve Donald
The moral right of the author has been asserted in accordance with
the Copyright, Designs and Patents Act 1988

ISBN 1-84299-003-9
Previously published by Barrington Stoke Ltd under ISBN 1-902260-14-7

Printed by Polestar AUP Aberdeen Ltd

Meet The Author - Terry Deary

What is your favourite animal?
A rat
What is your favourite boy's name?
Marmaduke
What is your favourite girl's name?
Bertha
What is your favourite food?
Horse
What is your favourite music?
Bagpipes
What is your favourite hobby?
Singing to bagpipes

Meet The Illustrator - Steve Donald

What is your favourite animal?
A goldfish
What is your favourite boy's name?
Kieran
What is your favourite girl's name?
Elizabeth
What is your favourite food?
Scrambled eggs
What is your favourite music?
'70s pop music
What is your favourite hobby?
Playing on my computer

For Rebecca Randall
with all good wishes

Contents

Streatley, Berkshire, England

1937

Ghosts are supposed to be scary things.
They shock and terrify the people who see
them. So why do so many people actually try to
see a ghost? Visitors flock to haunted castles,
book rooms in haunted hotels and even try to
buy a haunted piece of furniture ...

Chapter 1
Mrs Rundle's Brainwave

Mr Rundle sat at the breakfast table of *The Dog and Duck*. He noisily drank a cup of tea, chewed at a piece of toast and studied the adverts on the back page of the newspaper. Mrs Rundle sat opposite and read the headlines on the front page.

"I see the Chinese are sending 300,000 troops to fight the Japanese," she said.

"Very nice, dear," her husband replied.

Mrs Rundle blinked. She frowned. "I do wish you'd listen when I'm talking to you," she snapped.

"Yes, I read it in the paper."

Mrs Rundle buttoned up her cardigan fiercely. "There is a large hairy spider crawling up your nose to eat your brain!" she said.

"Really, dear?"

"But it's run out because it can't find any brains in there."

"Ah, that'll be right dear," Mr Rundle nodded and turned the page.

"I've put poison in your tea," she went on sweetly.

"Good grief!" the man cried suddenly.

Mrs Rundle jumped. "I was only joking. I only said it to make you sit up and listen!"

"Would you believe it?" he gasped.

"Believe what?" the flustered Mrs Rundle said.

"It's Mrs Barclay over at Carterton Manor!" he cried.

"What's she done now?"

"Placed an advert in the paper!"

"How exciting," Mrs Rundle sighed.

"No, listen! It says ...

FOR SALE – Haunted wardrobe. I will be glad to deliver this to anybody interested, complete with ghost. The ghost will be more at home if it is made to feel welcome. Please write to Mrs Barclay, Carterton Manor, Oxford."

"I always thought she was a funny woman," Mrs Rundle said.

"She's a wonderful woman and so charming, you said. Even though she has enough money to buy half of Oxfordshire," her husband reminded her and lowered the newspaper. He stuck a pipe in his mouth and tried to light it without setting fire to his huge and curling moustache. There was less chance of him setting alight to his hair because he had very little.

"Buy it, Mr Rundle," his wife ordered.

The man opened his mouth and his pipe almost fell into his teacup. "What on earth for?"

"We're having this inn rebuilt, aren't we? It'll add interest to *The Dog and Duck*. People will come from miles around to stay in a room with a haunted wardrobe," she told him. She folded her fat arms and dreamed.

"Where do we put it while *The Dog and Duck* is being rebuilt?" asked her husband.

"In the shed at the bottom of the garden. I'll phone Mrs Barclay now before somebody snaps it up," Mrs Rundle announced. "You can do the washing up."

Chapter 2
A Bargain Buy

Mrs Barclay of Carterton Manor was a small, neat woman. She wore a flowered dress and her grey hair was set in waves. She opened the door carefully. Her face brightened when she saw it was the Rundles.

"Oh, my dears, do come in!" she cried in a high voice.

"You are answering the door yourself, Mrs Barclay?" Mrs Rundle said.

"We've no servants!" Mrs Barclay sighed. "They've all left because of this ghost business. Martha, the cook, is threatening to go now. She says she can't stand any more. But come in and have a look at the wardrobe."

Mrs Rundle tugged at her husband's sleeve and pulled him towards the stairs which Mrs Barclay was already climbing. "A beautiful wardrobe," she said over her shoulder as she led the way. "I bought it in a sale three years ago. It was perfectly ordinary-looking. But I liked it and bought it. Only cost me ten pounds."

"Oh, Mr Rundle will give you twice that," Mrs Rundle told her. "Won't you, Mr Rundle?"

"Why not make it thirty?" her husband grumbled.

Mrs Barclay paused at the top of the stairs. "So many offers, you wouldn't believe it! First came the phone calls and today the letters

began to arrive. I'll show them to you if you like. But have a look at the wardrobe first."

She led the way into the bedroom. Mrs Rundle looked around wide-eyed. She admired the rich carpet, the wallpaper and the satin bedspread, but a layer of dust covered the bedside table.

"You've lost your cleaning maids too, I see," she said.

"Everyone has left and all because of this!"

Chapter 3
Mrs Barclay's Story

They stared at the wardrobe, a tall piece of furniture made of walnut. It had drawers and mirrors but looked no different to a thousand other wardrobes.

"It'll look nice in the best bedroom at *The Dog and Duck*," Mrs Rundle smiled.

"It'll attract guests for you," Mrs Barclay said with a tinkling laugh. "Judging from the interest my advert has received."

"That never crossed our minds," Mrs Rundle lied.

"I'll show you some of my letters," Mrs Barclay offered. She led the way into the living room, sank into an armchair and rang a bell. A woman with a white apron came out from the kitchen. She scowled at Mrs Barclay. "Tea for three, please Martha," Mrs Barclay said.

Martha, the cook, went back to make it. Mrs Barclay said, "We had no trouble for two years. Then guests began to ask about the wardrobe. *Was there something odd about it? Why did the doors keep opening and shutting? Would we mind if they went home?* Why, my dear, at this rate I'll have no friends left."

"Did you see anything for yourself?" Mr Rundle asked.

"Oh, yes. My butler, Mr East, and I spent an evening there. We checked it on the outside for secret panels and springs. Nothing! But when Mr East announced he would look inside, the most terrifying thing happened. The door flew off its hinges, crossed the room and smashed the dressing-table mirror! I nearly fainted."

"I'd have died," Mrs Rundle fluttered.

"But the spirit had been wakened by now," Mrs Barclay continued.

"Risen from the grave," Mrs Rundle went on.

"From the grave! That's what Mr East said. Then, one night, a ghostly shape appeared from the wardrobe …"

Chapter 4
The Wardrobe Changes Hands

"How big was it?" Mr Rundle asked.

"Almost eight foot!" said Mrs Barclay.

"What! An eight foot ghostly shape!"

"Sorry, I thought you meant the wardrobe," explained Mrs Barclay. "The ghostly shape was about five foot. It was a withered little man with one of those Sherlock Holmes hats ... a deerstalker, I think you call them."

"What did this ghostly shape do?" Mr Rundle asked.

"Walked down stairs and out of the front door," Mrs Barclay explained.

"Ghosts walk *through* doors," Mr Rundle said. Everyone knew that.

"Well this one didn't. He opened the door and slammed it behind him! Quite rude he was. What with banging doors, opening and shutting of the wardrobe doors, rattling noises, no one could get to sleep. The servants started to leave! The ghostly shape really disliked the butler and kicked him firmly on the shins. He left, of course."

"Can't blame him," Mr Rundle sighed.

"So the wardrobe has to go. Still, I never expected so many replies."

She pointed to the table in the centre of the room. Letters were sorted into neat piles. Mrs Barclay walked across to them and began to read parts of them.

"Look at this one ...

CAN I HAVE MY
MONEY BACK
IF THE GHOST
DOESN'T APPEAR?

"And this ...

*I am a professor
of ghostly studies...*

"And this ...

We are four ladies
living alone and we
think the ghost night
protect our house...

"And this ...

Do you think your
ghost would be happy
in a small modern
house?

"Well, the *ghost* might be but I doubt if the wardrobe would fit. And look at this!" Mrs Barclay cried and passed the letter to her friend.

Mrs Rundle read it and her jaw dropped at this insult. She read it to her husband.

Dear Mrs Barclay,
I am very interested in your wardrobe and you.
Will you marry me?

"Well I never! What a nerve!" said Mr Rundle.

"I've had lots of advice," Mrs Barclay went on.

Don't lock the wardrobe ...

place a nice
comfortable chair
beside the wardrobe
for the ghost.

There is almost
certainly treasure
inside ...

"And look at this ...

If I were you I'd
keep it. You'll
never have
another wardrobe
like that!

"I ask you!"

Mrs Rundle put the letters on the table and pushed them away from her. "*We'll* take it off your hands, won't we, Harry dear?"

"Er ... well ..."

"Harry will give you *fifty* pounds, won't you, Harry dear?"

"I'll deliver it to you tomorrow," Mrs Barclay promised. "I've had several calls from newspapers who want to spend the night with the haunted wardrobe," she said.

Chapter 5
Unwanted Visitors

The van pulled up at *The Dog and Duck* and Mrs Barclay pulled up behind in her Morris car.

"How did the ghost watching go?" Mrs Rundle asked as she watched three men carry the wardrobe to the shed at the bottom of the garden.

"Most strange," Mrs Barclay said. "We had reporters from two local newspapers and one of the London papers too."

"Oooh! You'll be famous!" Mrs Rundle sighed.

"Well they didn't want to take my photograph," Mrs Barclay sniffed. "They only wanted pictures of the wardrobe!"

"And did the little man appear? The one in the deerstalker hat?"

"Nothing happened for an hour," Mrs Barclay said in a low voice. Then she gripped Mrs Rundle by the arm. "Suddenly there were sounds from inside the wardrobe, sounds like berries falling off a tree. A reporter shone a torch on the floor and there was a button that had not been there before. Suddenly I saw him. 'He's there!' I cried. The little man came out of the wardrobe and ran across the room."

"Did the reporters see him?" Mrs Rundle asked.

"No," Mrs Barclay admitted. "They were just too slow." She looked down the garden path at the side of *The Dog and Duck* and watched as the shed door was closed.

"Well, I see it's found a safe home. I had so many offers ..."

"Oh! I mustn't forget to pay you," Mrs Rundle said and pulled fifty one-pound notes from the pocket of her overall.

"It's cheap at *twice* the price," Mrs Barclay said, tucking the money away deep inside her handbag. "You'll see. You won't be able to move for visitors to your inn."

But, when the visitors came, they were not the sort the Rundles wanted.

Chapter 6
Ghostly Goings-On

The wardrobe at the bottom of the garden didn't bother the Rundles ... but the visitors did. Mr Rundle was filling a glass with beer behind the bar when a young man with a large cap pulled down over his eyebrows ran into the bar.

"The ghost!" he wailed. "There's a ghost out there! It's horrible. Disgusting!"

The bar had been full. The young man had to step back to avoid being trampled in the rush to the door.

Another young man stood at the corner and panted, "The back garden. The shed! It came out of the shed wailing and screaming!"

The crowd from the bar elbowed each other out of the way to be the first to see the ghost. People in the same street came to their doors to find out what was going on. Soon there were fifty people crowded onto the back lawn of the inn.

It became strangely quiet. In the quietness a white shape appeared. It was tall and it flapped in the summer breeze. Some of the watchers backed away. Someone screamed.

The ghost began to make a sound that could only be described as ... ghostly.

"Hoooo! Hoooo!"

It had two large patches on the front of its head where eyes should have been. It turned towards the crowd on the lawn and began sliding towards them. Even the brave ones began to panic a little as the cries of the crowd and the wails of the ghost grew louder.

Suddenly the ghost fell forward. There was a ripping sound as it tripped on its sheet and the youth underneath the sheet fell flat on his face. He rolled over and hooted with laughter!

"Caw!" he cried. "You should have seen your faces!"

The angry crowd began to advance towards him. He dashed down the garden, past the shed and climbed over the wall that led to the railway line. He was still laughing as he ran off into the night.

Chapter 7
Things that Go Bump ...

"It's no use, Harry," one of the red-faced drinkers grumbled as he headed back towards the bar. "You'll be the victim of every joker in the county as long as you have that thing in the shed."

Mr Rundle sighed. "You're right. There's a room nearly finished upstairs. I'll bring it in first thing tomorrow."

But the Rundles suffered a restless night. Stones rained down on the roof of their shed. Voices hooted through the letter-box on their front door. Screeches and howls carried on until the early hours of the morning. The police had to be called to get rid of the jokers.

Next morning Mr Rundle, helped by some of his regular customers, dragged the wardrobe

48

into the inn and up the stairs to the best
bedroom.

A policeman on a bicycle patrolled the street.
The owners of *The Dog and Duck* looked forward
to a peaceful night.

But Mr Rundle woke with a start. He could have sworn that he had heard a rumbling from the wardrobe's new home that night. He slid his feet into an old pair of slippers and crept towards the door. Floorboards creaked under his feet but his wife snored peacefully.

He opened the bedroom door and it groaned like a dog with toothache. A little moonlight spilled onto the landing. Mr Rundle wished he'd brought a poker with him.

His mouth was dry and his bald head was beaded with sweat. He placed an ear against the door of the best bedroom. There were creaking noises that the old inn often gave in the stillness of the night, but nothing else.

When he pushed the door open something soft wrapped itself around his face. He almost screamed with fear. It was just a dressing gown hanging behind the door. The wardrobe was silent, but Mr Rundle felt it was the silence of a wild beast waiting to pounce.

He backed out of the room and padded back to the shelter of his bed. Maybe he just imagined the sound of laughter that followed him down the landing.

Chapter 8
Peace at Last?

Mr Rundle tried to laugh about it next morning when he told his wife about the noises.

"The ghost's looking for something, mark my words," Mrs Rundle told her husband.

"Yes, dear," the man said with a yawn.

"Take it apart and you may find the treasure," she said.

"Yes, dear."

"Well? What are you waiting for? Christmas?"

"You want me to do it *now*?"

The woman folded her arms. Mr Rundle understood what that meant. It took him an hour to take the wardrobe apart. It took him two hours to put it back together.

"No treasure," he reported.

And after that there was no ghost either. The disturbance seemed to have driven the little man in the deerstalker hat away.

"Fifty pounds is a lot to pay for a plain old wardrobe," Mrs Rundle complained a week later. The fuss had died down and the visitors had stopped coming to see it. "Why did you have to take it apart?" she demanded.

"Sorry, dear," Mr Rundle mumbled.

Mr Rundle read his paper. "There's a nice wardrobe for sale here ..." he began

Mrs Rundle folded her arms.

"Just a thought," her husband sighed.

Afterword

Some six months later Mr Rundle closed the bar for the night. He wiped the last table clean and went into the kitchen to make his cocoa. He climbed the stairs happily. Mrs Rundle was staying with her sister that week. He had to work harder in the bar, but at least he had a bit of peace after closing time.

Mr Rundle decided to sleep in the best bedroom. He slipped under the cool bed-sheets and supped the cocoa. He read the newspaper then folded it neatly and dropped it by the side of the bed. Then he wiped cocoa off his moustache and snapped the light off.

He sighed – he was a happy man. Only a faint light from a street lamp lit the room.

An owl hooted in the woods and a cat yowled in the garden.

A door creaked in the bedroom ...

Mr Rundle's drooping eyes flew open. In the half-darkness he saw the door of the wardrobe swinging outwards. He saw a tweed jacket. It could have been his own jacket hanging there – or it could have belonged to a little man in a deerstalker hat.

Mr Rundle didn't stay around long enough to find out. He spent the night in the kitchen with the coal fire blazing and all the lights switched on.

When the sun rose and the first bus arrived in the village his wife found him sitting at the table. There was a sheet of paper in his trembling hand. He'd managed to write just three words in a shaking hand:

Ghost for sale ...

What do you think?

Was there a ghost?

A furniture expert did report that the wardrobe showed signs of being altered – a new panel had been fitted into its floor. This could simply have replaced a damaged piece.

Had the ghost altered the wardrobe when he was alive and hidden something in that section?

Had someone else found this hidden 'something' and taken it away?

Was it money or was it something precious?

Is that why the grumpy little spook returned night after night?

We can only guess.

Can you explain it?

Was Mrs Barclay telling fibs about her wardrobe? Remember, the newspaper men never saw the ghost she claimed she had seen. Her servants were never interviewed and asked for their opinions.

The problem is, why would Mrs Barclay want to lie about the ghost?

Here is one possible explanation – one that *doesn't* involve ghosts, but which fits the facts.

Mrs Barclay needed money. (A lot of rich people lost money in the 1930s.) One by one the servants left because she couldn't afford to pay their wages.

She came up with an idea to make money. (It would not only bring her some cash – it would also explain to her nosy neighbours why the 'rich' woman had no servants.)

Mrs Barclay buys ten old wardrobes for (say) five pounds each. She places the advert for a 'haunted' wardrobe in the newspaper. She is flooded with offers. Many are willing to pay fifty pounds (or more) for a piece of junk worth a tenth of that. She sells the ten wardrobes to the ten highest offers. "This is the genuine, haunted wardrobe," she tells each one.

Result? She makes nearly five hundred pounds.

Possible? What do *you* think?

Who is Barrington Stoke?

Barrington Stoke was a famous and much-loved story-teller. He travelled from village to village carrying a lantern to light his way. He arrived as it grew dark and when the young boys and girls of the village saw the glow of his lantern, they hurried to the central meeting place. They were full of excitement and expectation, for his stories were always wonderful.

Then Barrington Stoke set down his lantern. In the flickering light the listeners were enthralled by his tales of adventure, horror and mystery. He knew exactly what they liked best and he loved telling a good story. And another. And then another. When the lantern burned low and dawn was nearly breaking, he slipped away. He was gone by morning, only to appear the next day in some other village to tell the next story.

If you loved this story,
why don't you read . . .

The Hat Trick

by Terry Deary

Is there something you'll remember
for as long as you live? Seaburn
football team meet their rivals and Jud
has to step in as goalie. They are two
goals down at half-time. How can
Seaburn recover?

Visit our website!
www.barrringtonstoke.co.uk